Cat and Dog

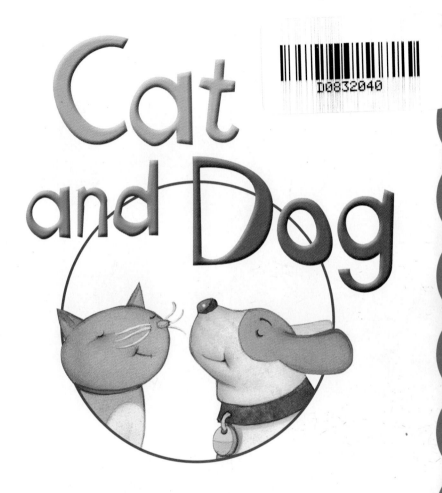

by Ada Mame
illustrated by Alan Flinn

 HOUGHTON MIFFLIN   BOSTON

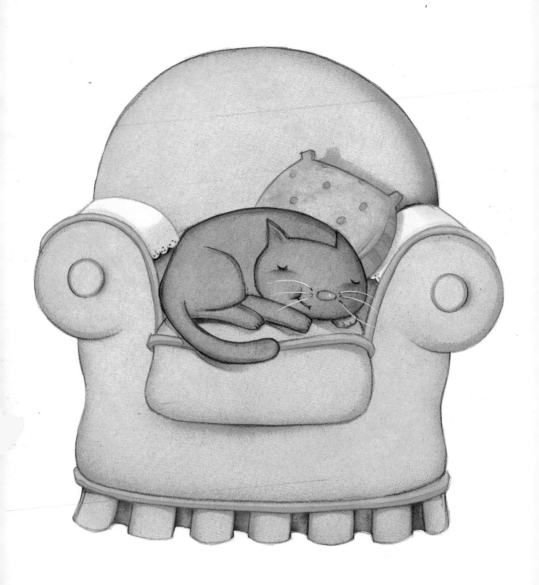

Cat is on the chair.

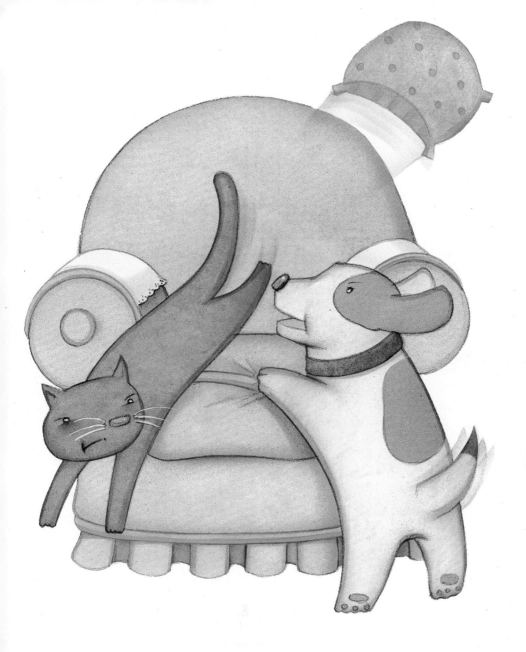

Dog wants to sit on the chair!

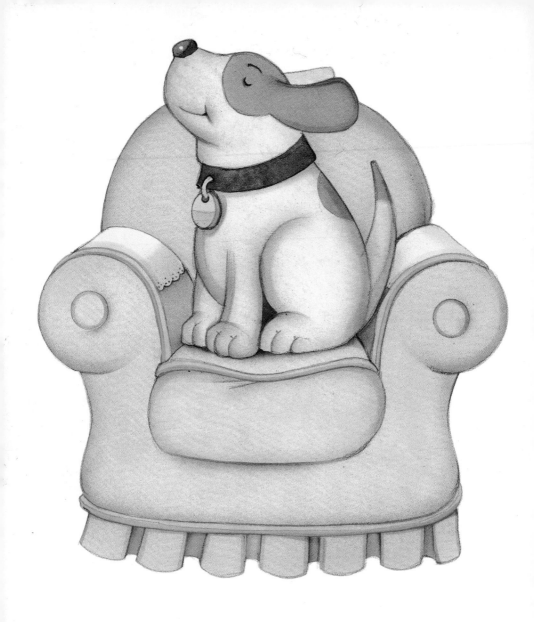

Dog is on the chair.

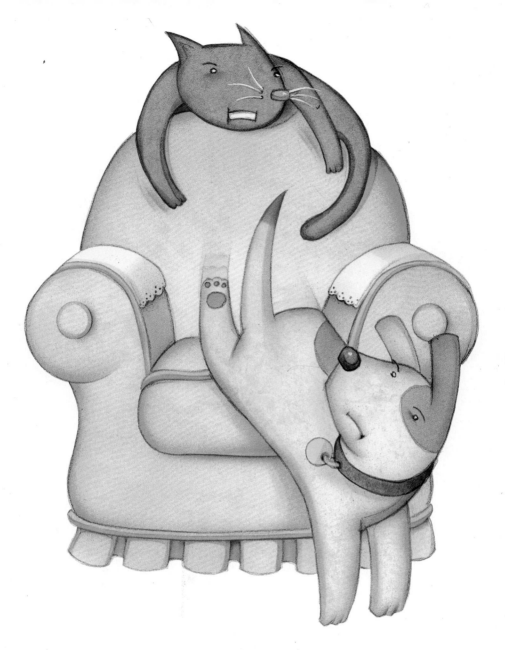

Cat wants to sit on the chair!

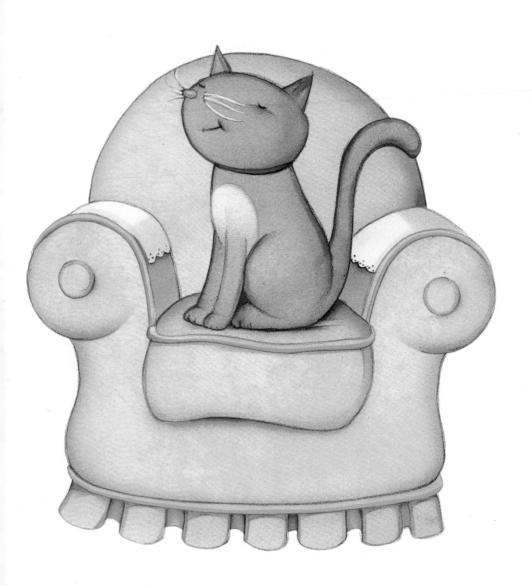

Cat is on the chair.

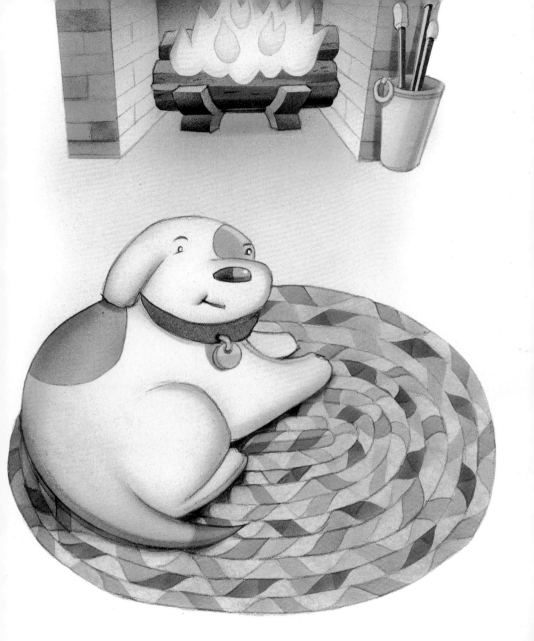

Dog is on the mat.

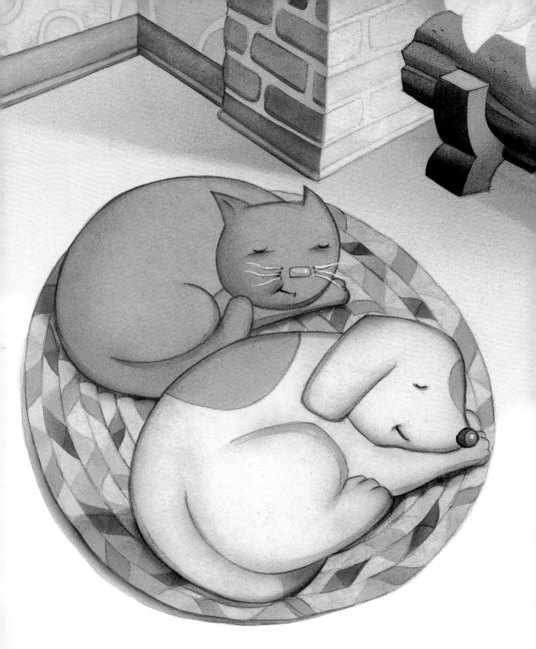

Dog and Cat are on the mat!